WHERE *Happiness* LIVES

WORDS
Barry Timms

LITTLE TIGER
LONDON

PICTURES
Greg Abbott

█████████████ his sweet little home.
He is happy and safe here, and never alone.

It has just enough room
    for each mouse to have fun,
And plenty of windows
    that let in the sun.

There's a garden outside
with a shady oak tree.

"I'm lucky!"
says Mouse.
"This home's
perfect
for me!"

But one day, out walking,
Mouse spots a large door.
It belongs to a house
that is hard to ignore . . .

There's oodles of space,
and a balcony too!
The owner – a white mouse –
looks out at the view.

"Good morning,"
calls Grey Mouse.
"I live down the way,
In a sweet little home
that seemed fine
. . . till today.

But your home's
much bigger.
I wish mine was grand.
You must be the
happiest mouse
in the land!"

The mouse on the balcony heaves a big sigh.
    "I WAS happy once . . .
        then a house caught my eye.

From my favourite chair, I gaze up at its tower,
    And now I'm more jealous with each passing hour!

It's simply amazing – like nothing I've seen!"
    "Please show me," says Grey Mouse.
        "It sounds like a dream!"

So they scamper along, never pausing to look
At the glittering fishes that leap in the brook.

And they don't see
the dance two bright
butterflies share,

Or hear the soft birdsong,
or sniff the sweet air.

TO THE
MOUNTAIN

There's a mountain to climb
but the mice don't give in.
The house at the top
makes their furry heads spin . . .

It's a house like no other!
This home has it all:
A garden with fountains,
a banqueting hall,

A dome, and a spire —
both designed to impress!
The brown mouse who greets them
has jewels on her dress.

"Welcome!" she cries.
"Won't you please step inside?
There's lots to explore here
and I'll be your guide."

She serves them
fine pastries on
plates made of gold,

Then leads them
through hallways
past treasures
untold.

"The
games
room . . .

the
parlour . . .

And this is the dome where I gaze at the stars!"

my room for guitars . . .

"Oh my . . . !"
    sigh the other two mice in dismay,
The last of their happiness
    drifting away.
"We once were contented
    but now we feel poor.
The happiest mouse
    is the mouse who has **more**."

The brown mouse says nothing, but points to a stand
Where a telescope rests, looking over the land.

For that is a house
where true happiness lives!"

18

And there, through its lens, is a sweet little home.
It doesn't have fountains, a spire, or a dome.

It doesn't have treasures – there isn't the space –
But each little mouse has a smile on its face.

"It's lonely up here," says the wealthy brown mouse,
"But it brightens my day just to look at that house.

What a treasure it is! Oh, the joy that it gives . . .

"It's MY home!" cries Grey Mouse.
"Well, who would have guessed
That a mouse in a mansion
could think that I'm blessed!

Whatever your home,
it is happy indeed . . .

If you love what you have . . .

and you have what you need."

"How true!"
cheers the white mouse,
his eyes shining bright.
"I don't need a high tower.
My home is just right!"